D0495028

A Dose of Dr Dog

Babette Cole

A Tom Maschler Book
Jonathan Cape · London

Dr. Dog was
studying herbal
medicine and
having a nice
restful holiday . . .

. . . until his pesky family,
the Gumboyles, turned up.

"I suppose they will make themselves ill again and I'll have to look after them as usual," said Dr. Dog.

So he set
off into the
jungle to look
for herbal
medicines.

During his search he met the long-lost herbal scientist,
Professor Dash Hund.

The Professor was hunting for a rare and dangerous plant, the Nosenip Terriblanus.

NOSENIP TERRIBLANUS

RARE and dangerous child-eating plant. Sap from this family of Noseyparkerfondilitus could be used as a fossil fuel.!

He showed Dr. Dog his tropical herb garden
and explained the healing power of each plant.

At the back of the garden, Professor Hund
suddenly spotted a trail of nosenip slime.

"Oh no!" said Dr. Dog.

"It's leading
straight back to
the Gumboyle
camp."

"Oooh, aren't they sweet,"
said Ma, as Dr. Dog and
Professor Hund came
racing into
the camp.

"STOP PLAYING
WITH THEM
THIS MINUTE!"
said Dr. Dog. "They are
highly dangerous!"

But it was too late. Kurt stood in some nosenip poo.

The poo-flies bit him badly!

"These are mosquito bites," said Dr. Dog.

"Garlic juice will stop the itching," said Professor Hund.

They rubbed some on.
Kurt was very relieved.

Fiona had been sunbathing on a nosenip without any sun block!

"Silly girl," said Dr. Dog, "you are badly burnt!"

"Sap from an aloe plant will work wonders,"
said Professor Hund.

"Ooh, that's better," said Fiona.

Gerty had been skipping with
the nosenips.

She felt sick.

Yuck!

"Motion sickness is caused by your food sloshing about in your tummy," said Dr. Dog.

"A little ginger tea will settle that,"
said Professor Hund.

Kev had been bronco riding on a nosenip.
He sat on one of the spines . . .

. . . and got a
spot on his bot.

"That's not a spot," said Dr. Dog.
"It's a nice, juicy boil full of pus!"

OW!

"A paste of
dried marigold
petals will soon
draw it out,"
said Professor
Hund.

Very slowly, the
boil got bigger . . .

and bigger . . .

AND
BIGGER!

And very quickly, the
nosenips got hungrier . . .

and hungrier . . .

AND
HUNGRIER!

Suddenly one of them struck.

It got Baby Gumboyle!

Luckily, Kev's boil burst at that very moment.
The nosenip spat Baby out!

SPLOSH

Kev felt so
much better.

"Right, that's it," said Ma Gumboyle.
"We're NEVER going on holiday again!"

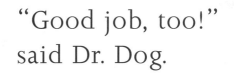

"Good job, too!"
said Dr. Dog.

To Dr. Dog

A DOSE OF DR. DOG
A JONATHAN CAPE BOOK 978 0 224 07057 7

Published in Great Britain by Jonathan Cape,
an imprint of Random House Children's Books

This edition published 2007

1 3 5 7 9 10 8 6 4 2

RANDOM HOUSE CHILDREN'S BOOKS
61–63 Uxbridge Road, London W5 5SA

www.**rbooks**.co.uk

Addresses for companies within The Random House Group Limited can be found at:
www.randomhouse.co.uk/offices.htm

THE RANDOM HOUSE GROUP Limited Reg. No. 954009

A CIP catalogue record for this book is available from the British Library.

Printed in Singapore